FAT CAMP COMMANDOS GO WEST

By DANIEL PINKWATER

Illustrated by ANDY RASH

A
LITTLE
APPLE
PAPERBACK

SCHOLASTIC INC.

New York   Toronto   London   Auckland   Sydney
Mexico City   New Delhi   Hong Kong   Buenos Aires

No part of this publication may be reproduced in whole or in part, or stored
in a retrieval system, or transmitted in any form or by any means, electronic,
mechanical, photocopying, recording, or otherwise, without written permission
of the publisher. For information regarding permission, write to Scholastic
Inc., Attention: Permissions Department, 557 Broadway, New York, NY 10012.

ISBN 0-439-29773-7

Text copyright © 2002 by Daniel Pinkwater. Illustrations copyright © 2002 by
Andy Rash. All rights reserved. Published by Scholastic Inc. SCHOLASTIC, LITTLE
APPLE PAPERBACKS, and associated logos are trademarks
and/or registered trademarks of Scholastic Inc.

12 11 10 9 8 7 6 5 4 3 2 1   3 4 5 6 7 8/0

Printed in the U.S.A.   40

First Scholastic paperback printing, April 2003

The text type was set in 15-point Coop Light.

Book design by Kristina Albertson
Cover illustration © 2002 by Andy Rash
Cover design by Andy Rash and Kristina Albertson

To Jill. Who Else?

I.

We were sitting on our suitcases
outside Deepdip Cha-cha's Fun Ashram
for Kids. It was hot. Dust blew in our
faces. A tumbleweed tumbled past.

"I can't believe our parents did this to
us," my sister, Sylvia, said.

"I can't believe it either," I said. My
name is Ralph – Ralph Nebula.

"It's not just that they did it – it's that they did it *again*," Sylvia said.

"We hated it the first time. We made that perfectly clear to them," I said.

"And yet they did it again," Sylvia said.

"And they lied about it," I said.

"That's true!" Sylvia said. "They knew if we knew they were about to do it again we would raise heck."

"Why do you suppose they did it?" I asked Sylvia.

"There's only one possible answer," she said.

"Our parents are stupid?" I asked.

"Can there be any other reason?"

"Does this mean we are going to turn stupid when *we're* adults?" I asked.

Sylvia didn't answer.

II.

A scorpion crawled past. Sylvia and I watched it until it was out of sight.

Sylvia and I are fat. We are fat kids. It was never a big deal. We never gave it a thought. Our parents are fat. We're a fat family. We were happy.

Then, our parents started listening to a guy named Simon Primly. Simon Primly's mission in life is to save all fat people. He wants to save them from being fat. He goes on television and saves fat people. He has made millions of dollars saving fat people. Most of them he doesn't save. Most of them he just annoys.

Our parents listened to him, and he made them feel all guilty because we, their kids, were fat. Simon Primly says our parents made us fat, because

1-800-55-JUMBO

they're fat, and now our lives will be
ruined.

We can't see how being fat will ruin our
lives. We are happy. We are good stu-
dents. We are good at sports. We have
friends. The only thing wrong with our
lives is that our parents are idiots. They
are idiots, and they listen to Simon Primly.

Last summer, they listened to Simon
Primly and sent us to Camp Noo Yoo.

4

Camp Noo Yoo is a fat-camp. It was run by a gym teacher named Dick Tator. We told them we didn't *want* to go. We told them we didn't *need* to go. We told them we didn't have a problem with being fat. They sent us anyway.

III.

A Gila monster passed by. We sat on our suitcases. It was hot. The sun beat down on our turbans.

Camp Noo Yoo was bad. They served shredded carrots all the time. Shredded carrots at room temperature. Shredded carrots with raisins. Dick Tator hollered at the kids. The lake was dried up. The kids would have starved, except you could buy pizza from Dick Tator's brothers. Even if a fat-camp were a good idea, Camp Noo Yoo would have stunk.

Then we met Mavis Goldfarb.

Mavis Goldfarb was a little, round fatball of fury.

Mavis had a plan.

"Let's blow this pop stand," Mavis had said to us.

"What? You mean just leave?"

"But . . . but . . . how can we? I mean, where would we go? Who would take care of us? What would we do?"

"We will go to my house. My parents are away for the rest of the summer. Shlermie, our gardener, butler, and man-of-all-work, will take care of us, and what we will do is strike a blow against prejudice, especially fat-prejudice."

Sylvia and I thought about the summer before, about how we had escaped from Camp Noo Yoo with Mavis and become social guerrillas, and fighters against fat-prejudice.

A coyote went past.

IV.

The sun shone down on the road outside Deepdip Cha-cha's Fun Ashram for Kids. It must have been 102°. Sylvia and I sat on our suitcases and sweated in our yoga suits. A sidewinder wound past.

It had been fun turning the tables on unthinking people in Pokooksie, New York, after we escaped from Dick Tator and Camp Noo Yoo. We talked loudly about skinny people right in front of them, as if they had no feelings. We went jogging wearing horizontal stripes and made fun of the skinny people who couldn't keep up. We called up Dr. Frizzbender, the local phony fat-doctor, and exposed him as a liar on a call-in radio show.

Old Shlermie, the Goldfarbs' man-of-all-work, took good care of us and prepared delicious meals. Mavis had a beautiful, big house. As far as our parents knew, we were still at Camp Noo Yoo. Dick Tator, the loudmouth gym teacher who ran Camp Noo Yoo, probably thought we were still there.

But we were back in Pokooksie, becoming expert prejudice-fighters. Then we got busted.

V.

A jackrabbit hopped past. We looked up the road. Not a car in sight.

Way in the distance, inside the gate of Deepdip Cha-cha's Fun Ashram for Kids, we could hear the kids chanting. They were sitting in rows, wearing their junior yoga suits and turbans, chanting.

**THE PICKLE IS OUR FRIEND
THE PICKLE IS OUR FRIEND
THE PICKLE IS OUR FRIEND
OHH-OHHH RAMA
THE PICKLE IS OUR FRIEND**

It was Officer A. John Pup who busted us. We had been altering a billboard in Pokooksie, New York. While we were adding forty pounds to the model in the bathing suit, he snuck up on us.

Officer Pup was a good cop. He was also a fan of operettas by Gilbert and Sullivan. He was also fat. He sentenced us to taking part in the summer production of *The Pirates of Penzance* presented by the Pokooksie Overweight Gilbert and Sullivan Society, of which all the members were fat, or else had to wear fat-suits when onstage. It was a good punishment.

We liked it. We also had to promise not to commit any more outrages. That was okay. We decided we'd rather be actors.

VI.

A raiding party of Oglala Sioux rode past. We recognized them by their costumes and the decorations on their ponies. We waved to them, and they gave us the "V" sign. "Better luck this time!" we shouted.

Of course, at the end of the summer, when Camp Noo Yoo ended and Mavis's parents came back from studying fossils in Africa, we more or less had to tell the adults what had been happening. Not to do so would have been lying, and besides, we wanted them to see us act in *The Pirates of Penzance*, even though we only had bit parts.

We explained to them that fat-camp had never done any good, and that it was okay to be reasonably fat if you were healthy and active. Besides, there was plenty of evidence that the chances of getting thin and staying that way were very, very, very, very small – and dieting was dangerous. Mavis had plenty of charts, and stuff she printed off the Internet.

We told our parents we didn't want to go to fat-camp anymore. All we wanted to do was act in Gilbert and Sullivan operettas.

They said they understood, and they all came to see us be pirates and policemen in *The Pirates of Penzance*.

VII.

A kangaroo rat hopped past. The desert shimmered in the heat of the sun. We drew lines in the sand with the toes of our sandals. We remembered.

It had all seemed settled and finished. Our parents met Mavis's parents and Shlermie. They knew that even though we had run away from Camp Noo Yoo we still had adult supervision, and we were never in any danger. Besides, Camp Noo Yoo was shut down by the Departments of Health and Conservation. They said it was not safe to have a children's camp on the shores of a dried-up lake that was now mostly quicksand. Also, the camp shared territory with the largest known population of endangered Mosholu rattlesnakes, and it was suspected that the camp kitchen had been serving them to the campers as food.

Our parents became friends with the Goldfarbs, Mavis's parents. Very often we would all go out to supper at Fu Man Chuck's Chinese-American Restaurant and Pizzeria. And, of course, we children continued as junior apprentices of the Pokooksie Overweight Gilbert and Sullivan Society. We all enjoyed it, but Mavis more than enjoyed it. Mavis was really talented. Mavis was really popular. Mavis was becoming a star. While Sylvia and I were still members of the chorus, dancing hornpipes, and singing things like "Taran-ta-ra, taran-ta-ra," Mavis was getting actual parts.

You have to consider that in an amateur operetta group of which more than half the members are female, and just about all the members are fat, getting the role of Buttercup in H.M.S. *Pinafore* would be a spectacular accomplishment for anyone, let alone a mere kid. Mavis got it. And of course she was great. The audience stamped and whistled after she sang, "I'm called Buttercup," and her picture was in the newspaper.

VIII.

We watched a small sandstorm
blow past in the distance.

Our parents had taken to spending a lot of time with
Mavis's parents. In addition to family meals at Fu Man Chuck's,
they attended cultural events together: movies, concerts, and
lectures. They went to a lecture by Deepdip Cha-cha, who was
a swami, and whose mommy was a swami. Deepdip Cha-cha
came from a long line of swamis. After the lecture, they
bought all the books by Deepdip Cha-cha, and a book by his
swami mommy, Chichi Cha-cha. Sylvia and I thought nothing of
this at the time.

Then we heard that Mavis's parents were going to study
the Komodo dragon when summer came, and Mavis was going
to a dude ranch out west, Rough-Ridin' Rudy's Rootin'-Tootin'
Rancho. Next, we heard that our parents were going to the
island of Komodo with Mavis's parents, to study the Komodo
dragon, too!

Mavis wanted us to go to Rough-Ridin' Rudy's Rootin'-

Tootin' Rancho with her, but Sylvia and I hesitated. We loved our friend Mavis, but she was . . . well, she was more interesting than we were. She had more ideas than we did. When we

first met her, she was a Celtic witch. We never found out what that was about. Then she was the one who thought of running away from Camp Noo Yoo. Then she led us in cultural protest and fat-prejudice fighting, and finally she was Buttercup, and we were part of the chorus of sailors.

We knew if we went to the dude ranch with her, she would be the only person who was able to ride Old Diablo, and we would be among the people sitting around the campfire singing "Ti-yi-yippee-yippee-yay!"

IX.

We saw a cloud of dust way off in the distance. It could have been a car, maybe coming our way.

"We have decided to go to Deepdip Cha-cha's Fun Ashram for Kids," we told Mavis. "Our parents found out about it. We will learn to meditate, and by the end of the summer we will have our Junior Swami certificates. It will be fun. We will

practice vegetarianism, and learn Indian dance, and chapati-making."

"I don't advise it," Mavis Goldfarb said. "I think you should come to Rough-Ridin' Rudy's Rootin'-Tootin' Rancho with me."

"Why? Don't you think we are able to pick a good place to go for a vacation?" we asked Mavis.

"I just think you won't like it once you get there," Mavis said. "You'll have more fun if you come with me."

"Our minds are made up," we said. "At the end of the summer, you will tell us all about what it was like at the dude ranch, and we will show you how we learned to levitate and hold our breath for twenty minutes."

"If your minds are made up, they're made up," Mavis Goldfarb said. She handed us a tiny cell phone. "Just take this with you, and promise you'll call me if there's an emergency."

"What kind of emergency could there be?" we asked her. "We're going to a place of peace and tranquility, where we will enjoy healthy food, and seek inner quiet, and the ability to move solid objects with the power of our minds alone."

"Just promise you'll call if anything goes wrong," Mavis said.

X.

The dust cloud got larger. It was a car. It would be in front of the ashram in half an hour or less.

There was the usual period of excitement, while our mother packed our magic crystals and sewed name tags in our dhotis, and then the great day came, and we set off for Deepdip Cha-cha's Fun Ashram for Kids.

The first thing we noticed was that all the other kids were fat. Then we visited the ashram bookstore and saw they had all the books by Simon Primly.

Next, we went to lunch, and there were the mounds of hated shredded carrots, with raisins, at room temperature.

As if we hadn't gotten the picture yet we saw who was managing the ashram. It was Dick Tator! The beard and turban didn't fool us a bit.

And then we read the letter from our parents. It was waiting for us when we got there. They loved us. They felt terrible about Camp Noo Yoo. But they still felt guilty. We were fat and it was their fault. They wanted to give us this one more chance to save ourselves from fatness and having our lives ruined.

"Great balls of goo!" Sylvia shouted. "They're still not cured! They've been reading Simon Primly on the sly!"

"And they've sent us to another fat-camp!" I wailed.

"Only this time there's curry powder in the shredded carrots," Sylvia said.

"Well, let's not wait around," I said.

"Right," Sylvia said. "You have the cell phone?"

XI.

The cloud of dust got closer and closer, and the car screeched to a stop. We recognized the Goldfarbs' Nash Rambler luxury limousine, sleek and shiny under a coating of desert dust. The door opened, and out stepped old Shlermie!

Shlermie was wearing the biggest cowboy hat we had ever seen, along with boots, spurs, a six-gun, and sheepskin chaps. For the rest, he had on his usual black butler suit, the vest, the little tie, and the white gloves.

"Howdy, little buckaroos," Shlermie said. "The boss lady sent me to fetch you soon as you called her on that cell phone contraption. Climb into the buckboard, and I'll carry you on back to the ranch."

"Gone totally western, huh?" we asked Shlermie.

"When in Rome, children," Shlermie said. "Shall we go?"

"Why didn't Mavis come with you?" we asked.

"Miss Mavis has to keep an eye on developments in the town of Horny Toad," Shlermie said.

"Horny Toad? Is that where Rough-Ridin' Rudy's Rootin'-Tootin' Rancho is?" we asked Shlermie.

"It is," Shlermie said. "And a rougher, tougher, more two-fisted, gun-shootin', fist-fightin', card-cheatin', cattle-rustlin', hootin', hollerin' town there ain't never been nowhere nohow."

XII.

"**How is** it Mavis brought you along on her vacation?" we asked Shlermie, once we were seated comfortably in the Nash Rambler.

"I came to cook for little Miss Mavis. Otherwise it's Cattle-Rustler Steak and Pancho Villa Beans every night at Rough-Ridin' Rudy's Rootin'-Tootin' Rancho."

"I bet it's a nice place," I said.

"See for yourself. Here we are!" Shlermie said.

"We've arrived?"

"Horny Toad!" Shlermie said.

"But we were hardly in the car fifteen minutes!" Sylvia said.

"And the scenery was great, don't you agree?" Shlermie said.

"How come we had to wait in the hot sun for hours?" we asked.

"I thought I was being followed on the way to get you," Shlermie said. "I had to be careful."

"Careful? Careful of what? Followed by whom?" we asked.

"Vigilantes, posses, bushwhackers, varmints, owlhoots, desperadoes, bad men, gunslingers, ornery galoots – there's a range war going on, you know."

"A range war?"

"Well, practically. Miss Mavis will tell you all about it."

#

"What do you suppose Shlermie is talking about?" I whispered to Sylvia.

"I have no idea," she whispered back. "He's completely into the whole western thing, and you know how he likes to play-act. He could be making stuff up."

"Eccentric in the head?"

"That's my opinion."

We were getting our first impression of Horny Toad through the car windows. It was a town that would disappoint you, even if you weren't expecting anything. There were some crummy buildings, and some crummy streets, a couple of crummy horses, and some crummy people shaking their fists at us.

"Shlermie," I said. "Is it my imagination, or are people cursing us, and making rude gestures, and spitting at us, and throwing hunks of earth at the car?"

"It's the turbans, Master Ralph," Shlermie said. "Perhaps it would be a good idea if you were to take them off. We don't want any bullet holes in the car."

"They don't like our turbans?"

"They're simple folk, Master Ralph."

I looked at Sylvia. Sylvia looked at me. We took off our turbans.

"This vacation is getting funner and funner," Sylvia said.

XIV.

Rough-Ridin' Rudy's Rootin'- Tootin' Rancho was even crummier than the town of Horny Toad, if that were possible. The buildings looked like they were ready to fall down. So did the horses that were standing around in a dusty corral. There was a vulture sitting on top of a dead cactus.

"This is a dude ranch?" we asked Shlermie. "People come here to have fun? They pay to come here?"

"Well, not so many have come here just

lately," Shlermie said. "Look! Here comes Miss Mavis!"

We heard Mavis jingling before we saw her. She was wearing spurs, a big cowboy hat with silver things on the band, and a whole cowboy suit – all in black – with plenty of silver decorations on it. And, she was carrying a coiled-up bull-whip, also black.

"Howdy, Ralph!" Mavis said. "Howdy, Sylvia!"

"Howdy," we said. "What goes on here? Shlermie says there's some kind of range war going on, this place looks like death on a cracker, and going through town, the people threw clods and horse doo-doo at the car. Got an explanation?"

Mavis hitched her thumbs in her gun belt. We noticed that instead of a six-shooter she had a bottle of chocolate Yoo-Hoo in the holster. "Well, partners, it's not a range war . . . yet. But it's dang close to being one, and I'm a-hopin' you all will help me prevent it."

"'Dang? A-hopin'? We-all? Have you gone nuts, or what?"

XV.

"I suppose I may have picked up a few local expressions in the time I've been here," Mavis said.

"Which is less than a week," Sylvia said. "You will recall we said good-bye to each other in Pokooksie on Saturday."

"And I want to say I have missed you both," Mavis said. "I'm glad you decided to join me."

"Deepdip Cha-cha's Fun Ashram for Kids is a fat-camp," I said.

"I thought it might be," Mavis said. "Of course, now I know a lot more about it. But you must be hungry."

"We had shredded carrots for break-fast."

"We'll get Shlermie to rustle us up some grub," Mavis said. "And I'll tell you what's going on. Then we'll meet Rough-Ridin' Rudy and the rest of the cowboys."

"Are they real cowboys?"

"You saw the horses?" Mavis asked.

"Yes."

"Are they real horses?"

"Well, for lack of a better word."

"Same thing with the cowboys," Mavis said. "Let me show you your rooms while Shlermie cooks."

Mavis had a whole bunkhouse to herself, and there were rooms for each of us with cow skulls and Indian blankets and cactuses in pots.

"Not too many guests are staying here at the moment," Mavis said. "I told Rudy we will change all that. You might want to look in the closets for some cowboy clothes. I'm going to help Shlermie make tortillas."

XVI.

Sylvia and I appeared in the little dining room wearing checkered shirts and jeans we had found hanging in our closets. Mavis and Shlermie were just carrying platters of food to the table.

We forgot to ask any questions, and Mavis forgot to tell us anything while we ate the best lunch we'd ever had. Up to now, Sylvia and I had known about tacos and burritos - and that was all the Mexican or Southwestern cooking we had ever had. Shlermie had made chicken with pumpkin seeds, and fiery salsa with chunks of lime in it, and amazing dishes with corn and a salad that tasted familiar and strange at once.

"This is incredible," I said.

"I am inspired by the local materials," Shlermie said.

"This isn't what the regular guests eat," Mavis said. "Rough-Ridin' Rudy gives them huge hunks of charred meat and chili that can do permanent damage."

"Would that be one of the reasons there's nobody staying here?" I asked.

"One of them," Mavis said. "Come over to this window and I'll show you another one."

We looked out the window. Across an open space, which was nothing but dusty dirt, was the main building of Rough-Ridin' Rudy's Rootin'-Tootin' Rancho. Sitting on the porch, with their boots up on the railing, were a bunch of old, fat, sloppy, worn-out-looking cowboys. Most of them were whittling on little sticks of wood. All of them were spitting. They needed shaves, and it looked like they needed baths.

"Rough-Ridin' Rudy and his friends," Mavis said.

"They look very . . . authentic," Sylvia said.

"Too authentic," Mavis said. "They're way behind the times."

"I'd say about one hundred years behind," I said.

"Exactly," Mavis said.

XVII.

"The town of Horny Toad used to be a bustling place," Mavis said. "There were a dozen dude ranches here. People would come from all over. They'd ride horses, and rope steers, and have square dances every night. Twice a day there would be a fake bank robbery, and a stagecoach holdup. Movie companies from Hollywood would come here to shoot westerns, and people could meet the big cowboy stars. In those days the studios would turn out a horse opera every three or four days. On Saturdays and Sundays, some of the Amerindian people from the pueblo would dress up as Plains Indians and ride through town shooting off their rifles and having their pictures taken with the tourists. The rest of the

time, they could make good money as extras in movies. It was great."

"What happened?" we asked.

"Television happened," Mavis said. "In the early days of TV, there was a really popular cowboy show. So the other TV networks copied it. Then they copied the copies. Then, it got so that there were fifty cowboy shows on television every week. And . . ."

"People got completely sick of it!" Sylvia said.

"That's what happened," Mavis said.

XVIII.

"And then what?" I asked.

"The town sort of fell apart. A few of the dude ranches stayed open, but not many people came. It got to be like you see here at Rudy's. The guests had to take turns riding the healthy horse. Instead of fake bank robberies, there was a guy who would come around and try to pick your pocket. It was dismal. Some of the dude ranches went out of business – someone was buying them up."

"Who?"

"Peachy Wahoo Wa-Wa was a female

western movie star. She was known as
the Cowgirl Queen.

   She bought up some of the failing
dude ranches. Of course, her real name
wasn't Peachy Wahoo Wa-wa."

   "What was it?"

   "Her real name was Chichi Cha-cha."

   "What? The swami mommy of Deepdip
Cha-cha from whose ashram we
escaped?"

   "Yep. Only this was before she became
a swami. Chichi Cha-cha and a few others
converted some of the dude ranches to
health ranches. People would come and
eat wheat sprouts, and do yoga, and take
avocado baths."

   "And go on diets!" Sylvia and I said.

   "Yes," Mavis said. "So it wound up that
Horny Toad didn't die. There were the
remaining dude ranches, and the newer
health ranches, or fat-camps. Only the
dude ranches never did really well

again – and the health ranches and ashrams and such never really got big. After all, you can see what a crummy-looking town it is. That's how it is today – and that's why there's trouble."

"That's why there's trouble? Why should that be why there's trouble?" we asked Mavis.

"Let's go over and meet Rudy and the cowboys," Mavis said. "Then you'll under-stand more of the story."

As we walked over the dusty dirt to the main building of the dude ranch, we asked Mavis, "Did you know about all this stuff before you came here?"

"Most of it."

"Did you know the dude ranch and the town were utter doo-doo?"

"Pretty much."

"Then why did you want to come here? And why did you try to get us to come here, which we seem to have done?"

"Oh, I had a special reason."

"Which was?"

"Tell you later. Let's meet Rudy and the boys."

XIX.

"Rough-Ridin'  Rudy, I'd like you to meet my friends, Ralph and Sylvia," Mavis said.

"Pleased to meet you, partners," Rough-Ridin' Rudy said. "These are my partners, the Jalapeño Kid . . . Kid, meet Ralph and Sylvia."

"Pleased to meet you, partners," the Jalapeño Kid said.

"Wild Bill Hockup," Rough-Ridin' Rudy said. "Wild Bill, meet Ralph and Sylvia."

"Pleased to meet you, partners," Wild Bill Hockup said.

"Six-Finger Jack," Rough-Ridin' Rudy said. "Six-Finger, meet Ralph and Sylvia."

"Pleased to meet you, partners," Six-Finger Jack said.

"Black Schwartz," Rough-Ridin' Rudy said. "Black Schwartz, meet Ralph and Sylvia."

"Pleased to meet you, partners," Black Schwartz said.

"The Urp brothers, Wilbur and Orville," Rough-Ridin' Rudy said. "Urps, meet Ralph and Sylvia."

"Pleased to meet you, partners," the Urps said.

"The Jalapeño Kid, Wild Bill Hockup, Six-Finger Jack, Black Schwartz, and the Urps are all retired lawmen or bad men," Mavis said.

"Some of us are both," one of the Urps said.

"Tell Ralph and Sylvia about the trouble," Mavis said.

"Oh, it's those dang-blasted, dad-gum healthies," Rough-Ridin' Rudy said. "They're driving away our customers."

"And how are they doing that?" Mavis asked.

"Well, you know, Miss Mavis," Wild Bill Hockup said. "You've seen them and their weird foreign ways."

"Tell my friends about it," Mavis said.

"It's like this," Six-Finger Jack said. "People come to places like this to have a real, authentic, genuine Western experience. They want to imagine it's the old days of the Pony Express, and the big cattle drives, and Indians, and gun-fighters, and bad women, and card games, and gold mines, and stagecoaches, and roundups, and all that sort of junk."

"What they don't want to see," Black Schwartz said, "is a bunch of pudgy city people, wearing spandex in all the colors of the rainbow, and flashy sneakers, with miniature stereos, and air-conditioned hats, jogging along the trail, chanting about how the pickle is our friend."

The Jalapeño Kid continued, "They don't want to see ladies in muumuus coming into town to buy loofahs, meditation cushions, and bottled water from France, and yogurt. People in our general store should be asking for sacks of beans, and bullets for their rifle, and coffee beans, and cans of beans, and chili beans, and pinto beans, and . . . beans."

"I saw a lady asking for blueberry bath soap," Wilbur Urp said.

"Oh, is the blueberry soap in?" Black Schwartz asked. "It's easy on the skin, and it smells pretty."

"Now, see what I'm talking about?" Rough-Ridin' Rudy said. "Those dad-gum, gosh-durned, consarned yuppie, yogi healthies are just ruining our authentic Old West atmosphere. And they're turning Black Schwartz, once the toughest man in Abilene, into a big, soft, blueberry-smelling sissy."

"Get the picture?" Mavis asked us. "The cowboys feel the health farms ruin the Old West picture, and that's why they don't get any guests at the dude ranches."

"What about dude ranch business falling off when the TV networks made so many western shows that the whole country got fed up?" Sylvia asked.

"Shush," Mavis whispered. "These guys are still in denial about that."

XXI.

The next morning, Mavis got Sylvia and me to put on our yoga suits and turbans, wrapped a bath towel around her head, and hustled us into the Nash Rambler at dawn.

Shlermie drove us to the whole-grain pancake breakfast at the Friendly Zucchini Holistic Retreat and Organic Duck Farm. We were going to get the health-nut point of view.

The pancakes were pretty good. The healthoids talked about little other than the cowboys - we didn't need to ask any questions.

"Their horses go everywhere."

"They are scruffy and scuzzy."

"They smoke and chew tobacco."

"They're loud and obnoxious."

"They disturb my inner calm."

"They eat meat."

"They don't bathe."

"And worst of all, most of them are fat!"

"Oh, yes! Don't you just hate a fat cowboy?"

"And think of the poor horses!"

"Those cowboys look like overgrown gorillas."

"They're a blot on the landscape."

"No, they're blobs on the landscape!"

Sylvia whispered, "If there's going to be a war, I think I want to be on the side that's against these types."

"We're going to prevent the war," Mavis whispered. "So we have to over-look things ignorant people say."

Never had we known Mavis Goldfarb

to let an instance of fat-prejudice go unchallenged. Whatever she was up to, it was obviously very important to her.

XXII.

Back in the bunkhouse, we talked things over.

"So the cowboys blame the healthies, and the healthies blame the cowboys, because their respective businesses aren't doing all that well," I said.

"And no one admits that it's just a second-rate area for dude-ranching and health-ranching," Sylvia said. "And they'll never get a whole lot of people coming here."

"What they're missing," Mavis said, "is that while this isn't the greatest place to put a dude ranch or a health farm, there is one thing this town has got that no other town has got."

"What's that?" we asked Mavis.

"There is a reason for more people to come here than ever came here in the good old days. In fact, there is a reason for more tourists to come here than Disneyland, Las Vegas, Hollywood, and Washington, D.C, . . . combined."

"And what is that reason?" we asked Mavis.

"This reason is so compelling that if it were known – for example, if we got on the Internet and left a lot of posts around telling this reason – the town would fill up in a week, and there wouldn't be a room empty, plus people would be sleeping in tents and in their cars."

"What is the reason?" we shouted. "Tell us already!"

"The reason . . ." Mavis Goldfarb began.

"Yes?"

"The reason . . ."

"Yes, yes, yes?"

"The reason the town of Horny Toad is potentially the hottest tourist destination on the face of the earth is . . . can you guess?"

"We're going to throw you down and sit on you if you don't tell us!"

"Flying saucers!" Mavis cackled.

"Flying saucers?" we asked.

"Yes! Flying saucers! They're coming here!"

"Flying saucers? Little green men? Like on television?" we asked.

"Flying saucers, UFOs, extraterrestrials, little green men, little gray men, close encounters . . . this is where you have the best chance to see them, and . . . this is where they're going to land."

"So . . . it's like Roswell, where all the UFO crazies go?"

"It's fifty times better than Roswell."

XXIII.

"**Who knows** this besides you?" we asked Mavis.

"Shlermie. Shlermie knows. And now you know."

"That makes four people," I said. "This does not exactly suggest a stampede of space fans coming to Horny Toad."

"Which is why you, Ralph, and Shlermie are on your way to Pecos Printing and Cowboy Copies to have a few thousand fliers run off. And Sylvia and I are heading for the Horny Toad Public Library and Dance Hall to use the computer. We have to leave posts in hundreds and hundreds of chat rooms."

"So! You have a plan," I said.

"I always have a plan," Mavis said. "Now, be on your way – August sixth approaches."

"August sixth?"

"The day the extraterrestrials land here. We haven't got much time, so get busy."

"August sixth? August sixth is the day after tomorrow! How do you know it's going to be August sixth?"

"I know things. Go make copies."

"If lots of people come here, and no extraterrestrials show up on August sixth, won't they be mad?"

"They may be mad, but they'll be here," Mavis said.

XXIV.

We had 500 THEY'RE COMING! and 500 AUGUST 6TH fliers printed, and pasted them up all over town. We used kite string to tie them to cactuses to avoid putting tacks into them.

When Shlermie and I got back to the bunkhouse, Mavis was working on a drawing. "I have to go back to the library to relieve Sylvia. She's been spreading the word on the Internet for hours. Take this drawing to Rough-Ridin' Rudy, and talk him and the cowboys into building this in the desert just south of town."

"What is it?" I asked. The drawing looked like one of those stages they have at outdoor rock concerts.

"It's a stage," Mavis said. "You know, like

the ones they have at outdoor rock concerts. If they can rig some lights that run off car batteries, and some speakers, that would be cool."

"What reason do we give them for doing what looks like a lot of work?" I asked.

"Tell them it will save their flea-bitten, saddle-sore behinds," Mavis said. "Oh, and have them put up signs all over the place: NEUTRAL ZONE: NO SIX-SHOOTERS, NO TAI CHI STICKS."

XXV.

By the time Shlermie and I got back from persuading Rough-Ridin' Rudy and the rest of his cowboys to build a stage out in the middle of nowhere, Mavis and Sylvia were in the bunkhouse, waiting for us.

"Did you get all your posts out on the Internet?" I asked.

"The library closed. What we did will have to be enough," Mavis said. "Now you have to rehearse, Ralph and Sylvia."

"We have to rehearse?"

"Yes, you do. You have to learn a routine. It's important."

"What kind of routine?" we asked.

"A little song – maybe a few dance moves. It will be easy," Mavis said. "And you have to do it tomorrow night."

"On the outdoor stage the cowboys are building?"

"Yes."

"Funner and funner," Sylvia said.

XXVI.

The next morning there were already some tents and shiny Airstream trailers not far from where the cowboys were building the outdoor stage. All day long, people in old Volkswagen buses and on motorcycles turned up. There were a lot of people wearing sandals, guys with beards, and women with long hair.

A lot of the people had experience waiting for UFOs in the desert. Some of them set up outdoor kitchens, folding tables and chairs, and created little restaurants. I smelled yams, corn-on-the-cob, falafel, and tofu hot dogs cooking. Other people were selling telescopes, books about how to recognize aliens, and special pillows so your neck wouldn't get sore looking up.

There were tents set up like little theaters – you could go in and see a slide show about our neighbors from other planets. There were psychic doctors who could cure any disease by rubbing your feet, people who would make you a special aluminum-foil hat so your brain waves could not be interfered with, people selling books they had written about the times they were abducted by space aliens, people with flashing lightbulbs on their heads, and people made up like Klingons.

Also, in addition to the tents and trailers, there were teepees, hogans, yurts, and even underground burrows. A little weird city was taking shape. It was the neatest thing I had ever seen.

XXVII.

"**I guess** the word is getting around," Sylvia said.

"More people are showing up every hour," I said.

"Oh, and they are taking it seriously," Mavis said. "Have you seen all the gray four-door sedans, each with four guys wearing white T-shirts and Bermuda shorts? Those are government men – just in case there's really going to be a landing. And the ones with American flag T-shirts and sandals with socks? Those are foreign spies. This is turning into quite a party."

"What will happen when no spacemen show up?" I asked. "Won't people be mad?"

"Be optimistic," Mavis said. "What if the

spacemen do show up? Think how happy everyone will be."

XXVIII.

"I would like you to promise me something," Mavis said.

"Sure. What is it?" Sylvia and I asked.

"Tonight, after you sing your song . . ." Mavis began.

"You're not making us go through with that?"

"You have to do it. It's very important. We have to promote an atmosphere of peace and tranquility."

"And singing a song will do that?"

"Yes. Now, listen. After you sing your song, you have to promise to make your way through the crowd, climb up that little hill, and hide in the bushes. Shlermie will be waiting there, with binoculars. You'll be able to see what happens and hear what comes over the loudspeakers on the stage."

"All the way over there? And why hide in the bushes? This sounds crazy," we said.

"It's not crazy. It's your good friend asking you to make a solemn promise. Will you do it?" Mavis seemed serious.

"Well, all right, but it sounds completely wacky."

"Things are going to happen tonight that you don't know about – and I want you to be witnesses," Mavis said.

"What sort of things? All along you haven't been telling us everything you know. What's really going on? Can't you tell us?"

"I really can't," Mavis said. "It isn't that I don't trust you. I promised not to tell anyone. Even Shlermie doesn't know. Just do as you promised."

XXIX.

Sylvia and I wandered through
the now huge encampment in the desert.
Even more tents, and trailers, and wig-
wams, and wickiups, and lean-tos, and
booths, and buses had arranged them-
selves in rows. There were streets
where there had just been a couple of
lizards the day before.

It was like a county fair. People had set
up endless shops and concessions. They
were selling potatoes from the moon,
UFO dowsing sticks, books about visitors
from other planets, space helmets, special goggles that would allow you to pick
out aliens from among ordinary Earth-
citizens, frozen and microwaved Milky Way
bars, those green glow sticks, astronaut
ice cream, and deep-fried Oreo cookies.

In addition to selling things, there were

also quite a few exhibits. You could pay two dollars to squint through a little window in the side of a truck and see a dead Martian. There was the world's largest chicken, though I couldn't see what that had to do with visitors from space. And there were antennae, shrines, light arrays, and landing pads.

There were people strolling through the streets of the encampment, strumming guitars and electronic harps, and playing nose flutes. Space music could be heard coming from tape decks in some of the concessions. The good smells of all the things cooking mixed together with whiffs of interplanetary incense. People played games like Saucer Toss, and Rings of Saturn, and Whack-a-Martian. And all the while we heard the sound of hammering as Rudy's cowboys hurried to finish the stage.

The events in the desert were not wasted on Rudy and the cowboys. At some point they had run home and spray-painted their ten-gallon hats and

cowboys boots with silver radiator paint.
They had also painted a sign and nailed it
to the stage under construction:

THIS STAGE COURTESY OF RUDY'S SPACE RANCH.

The cowboys had disintegrator
blasters, bought from one of the ven-
dors, in place of their six-shooters. They
had dragged the portable barbecue
from the ranch and were selling Plutonian
chili and galactic steaks.

Chichi Cha-cha, formerly Peachy Wahoo
Wa-wa, swami mommy of Deepdip Cha-cha
and proprietress of several leading
health and spiritual growth establishments
in town, including Deepdip Cha-cha's Fun
Ashram for Kids, from which we had
recently escaped, was personally
conducting a Welcome-Our-Galatic-
Neighbors meditation in a big tent.
It cost two dollars to get in.

I heard someone say that the town
of Horny Toad had not had such a busy

day since Hopalong Cassidy's bar mitzvah.

XXXI.

"Horny Toad is back on the map," I said to Sylvia.

"What happens when the spacemen don't show up?" Sylvia asked. "Won't people get mad and go away?"

"I don't think so," I said. "Everyone seems to be having a good time. Besides, I keep hearing rumors that they are already here, disguised, and mingling with the crowd."

"It would be pretty difficult to pick out who's an alien," Sylvia said.

Mavis appeared. "I've been looking all over for you," she said. "You have to be onstage, just as it gets dark."

"Right, Mavis. We've got it covered. We'll be there."

"And you remember your promise to me?"

"Go hide in the bushes as soon as we finish our number," Sylvia and I said. "We remember. But how about an explanation? And how long do you want us to hide there?"

"It would take too long to explain," Mavis said. "I still have to go around organizing the dude-ranchers and healthies to take advantage of the outer-space theme. It will all be perfectly clear to you once you're in your hiding place. Just trust me. You do trust me, don't you?"

"We trust you, of course. But it would be more interesting if we knew what was going on."

"It will be interesting," Mavis said. "I can promise you the most interesting night of your lives."

XXXII.

"Do you think she means it?" I asked Sylvia.

"She's been acting all along as though there were really going to be space aliens," Sylvia said. "But she couldn't know such a thing, could she?"

"I don't see how," I said. "Unless she has been in secret communication with extraterrestrials. It seems more likely she has some kind of elaborate hoax or stunt in the works."

"That's what I think, too," Sylvia said.

"Let's go back to Rudy's Space Ranch and get our costumes on," I said. "It's getting to be evening."

XXXIII.

As the day drew to a close, the crowd in the desert became more and more excited. People were setting up their telescopes and dish antennas, pointed every which way. The new-age types were burning incense by the handful, meditating, ringing chimes, and chanting. Others were dancing around bonfires. Still others had earphones clamped on their heads and were tuning for radio signals. Many people were simply looking upward, their hands shading their eyes, waiting, waiting for some sign of the visitors from space.

Everybody seemed to understand that if they came it would be at night. As it got closer to sundown fewer and fewer vehicles turned up, until finally there were no more arriving. It was as though everybody who was coming had come. Then one more – the last one – a bus with the words FLASHIMOTO TOURS painted on the sides, carrying twenty or twenty-five fat men with horn-rimmed glasses, pulled in.

The fat men rushed out of the bus and began taking pictures of everything in sight. They were wearing plaid shorts and had white pudgy legs and leather loafers on their pudgy feet – no socks. There was a flurry of flashes as they photographed the tents, the buses, the variety of shacks, sheds, lean-tos and other temporary structures, the stage, the various UFO fans, the cowboys, the yogis, the Plutonian chili cooking in its pot, the sky, the desert floor, a dog, an abandoned sneaker, Rough-Ridin' Rudy, a Popsicle stick, a cactus. . . . Then, in less than five minutes, they quit taking pictures and piled back into the bus. Interesting, but only mildly so. They were

far from the strangest people we had
seen that day.

XXXIV.

Rudy and his cowboys were
singing cowboy songs on the stage. Six-
Finger Jack was quite an impressive gui-
tar player, which made sense considering
his natural advantage.

The crowd drifted toward the stage.

I ride an old paint, I'm leadin' old Dan
I'm goin' to Montana just
to throw the houlihan,
They feed in the coulees,
they water in the draw.
Their tails are all matted,
their backs are all raw.
Ride around, little dogies,
ride around them slow,

**For they're fiery and snuffy
and rarin' to go.**

The crowd sang along, and moved closer to the stage. Someone switched on the spotlights, and the cowboys were bathed in a golden glow.

**There was blood on the saddle,
blood all around.
And a great big puddle of
blood on the ground.
The cowboy lay in it
all covered with gore.
He'll never ride tall
in the saddle no more.
Oh, pity the cowboy,
all bloody and dead.
A bronco fell on him and
mashed in his head.**

Mavis appeared. "It's almost dark, kids. The moment of truth. I'll introduce you. Take your places."

XXXV.

The desert night was beautiful.
There was a wonderful smell. I guessed
it was sagebrush. There were about a
billion stars. The crowd of UFO crazies
was swaying and singing along with Rudy
and his cowboys. I don't know how many
people were there – it must have been at
least 2,000. The couple dozen fat guys
who had come in the Flashimoto Tours
bus were right down in front of the
stage. They all had on brightly colored
plastic ponchos that reached down to
their feet. They had big smiles on their
faces, and looked as though they were
having a really good time.

Mavis appeared on the stage. She was
wearing her big cowboy hat and black-
and-silver outfit.

"Ladies, gentlemen, and visitors from

other planets!" she said. "Welcome to the first space encounter in Horny Toad. In a little while, we can greet our guests from another world. But first, please welcome my two very best friends, with an important message in song. I give you, Ralph and Sylvia!"

Sylvia and I walked out to the center of the stage. Sylvia had a cowgirl suit on, and I was wearing my yogi suit and turban from Deepdip Cha-cha's Fun Ashram for Kids. We bowed and sang the song Mavis had taught us.

The health nut and the cowboy
should be friends,
Oh, the health nut and the cowboy
should be friends.
One likes to ride the range,
the other likes whole grains.
But that's no reason that
they can't be friends.
Horny Toad folks should stick together,
Horny Toad folks should all be pals.
Health nuts dance with
the cowboys' daughters,
Cowboys dance with
the health nuts' gals.

We bowed to each other, and did the dance steps we had rehearsed, and ended with the little curtsy with our fingers pointing to our chins, just as Mavis had instructed us.

Sylvia whispered to me, "I am never going on vacation with Mavis Goldfarb again."

XXXVI.

We got a reasonable round of applause, considering what a dopey exhibition we had just put on, got off the stage, and made our way through the crowd and up to the little hill. We found Shlermie crouching in the bushes.

"Here I am, Miss Sylvia and Mister Ralph," he said. "Miss Mavis said you'd be along, and here are binoculars for each of you."

"Do you know what this hiding in the bushes is all about?" we asked Shlermie.

"Not precisely," he said. "But Miss Mavis was quite insistent. She said we were not to leave our hiding place until it was all over, no matter what."

"Until what is all over?" we asked.

"I haven't the foggiest idea," Shlermie said.

"Just tell us this," I asked Shlermie. "In your opinion are there actual extraterrestrials involved in this, and if there are, how would Mavis know?"

"I believe she really thinks they will turn up," Shlermie said. "As to how she would know that, I can tell you that she has a subscription to *Popular UFOs* magazine and reads it cover to cover."

"Look!" Sylvia said, looking through her binoculars. "Mavis is back onstage and has the microphone."

"Cowboys, cowgirls, health nuts, and flying saucer crazies! The moment is at hand! They are among us! It is my supreme honor to present to you . . . Captain Rolzup of the Galactic Alliance and his senior staff!"

The two dozen fat guys bounded up on the stage, whipped off their plastic ponchos, and walked around with their hands clasped over their heads, like wrestlers

on TV. They were wearing silver jump-
suits and boots.

"I don't believe this," I said. "She's got
a bunch of fat guys in silver suits up
there, and she's trying to pass them off
as spacemen. The crowd will kill her!"

"Yaaaay!" the crowd said. It came
across louder than the loudspeakers. We
could feel the ground vibrate under our
feet. "Yaaaaaay! Yaaaaaay! Rolzup! Rolzup!
Rolzup!"

"They're buying it! I don't believe it!" I
said.

Sylvia, Shlermie, and I squinted through
the binoculars. Rolzup and his spacemen
were waving to the crowd. The people
were still going crazy, jumping up and
down and waving green glow sticks in the
air. "Rolzup! Rolzup! Rolzup!"

XXXVII.

Rolzup and his men took things out of their pockets. Through the binoculars we could see they were tiny instruments, like little pocket-sized saxophones and guitars. Then they blew into them and inflated them – blew them up like balloons. Then they began to play them! They sounded great!

I cannot begin to describe the music that Rolzup and his spacemen played. It was sweet and bouncy and loud, but not too loud, and it was very hard not to get up and dance to it. The crowd was doing just that. They were dancing up a storm. Mavis was dancing on the stage with the fat spacemen. It was a great concert!

They played for about half an hour. When they stopped I felt fantastic! Energized! Wired! Pumped-up! Alert! I

knew the crowd felt that way, too – and Sylvia, and even Shlermie!

Then, Rolzup held up his hands for silence. The crowd got quiet immediately. Rolzup made a speech.

"People of Earth! We are having a good time. It's nice to visit you again, as we have done so many times before. We want to thank the people of Horny Toad, and our friend Mavis Goldfarb, for making us welcome."

Mavis? He was thanking Mavis? Why was he thanking Mavis? I caught myself believing that they were really extraterrestrials and not just an extremely good band made up of fat Earth-guys. I shook my head, trying to clear my thoughts. Why shouldn't he thank her? There was no evidence they had come from space. They hadn't done anything that Earth-people couldn't do.

"And now," Rolzup said, "we have to go.

Please look to the skies, and you will see the Mother Ship." Rolzup pointed upward. High in the sky, I could see a green object, glowing. It appeared to be descending, getting closer.

It got closer and closer. It was squar-ish and oblong. I looked through the binoculars. It was the Flashimoto Tours bus! No! It was a bus - well, it looked like a bus - but it was bigger. It was much, much bigger! It was really big! It was immense! It was colossal!

It hovered above us. It had to be a mile long. It looked exactly like a bus, a mile-long bus.

XXXVIII.

"**Before we** are transported to the
ship, my associates will pass among you
and squirt you with a harmless aerosol."

As he spoke, the fat spaceguys ran
through the crowd with truly amazing
speed, and squirted each and every person in the nose with little atomizers,

which they worked by squeezing a rubber
bulb. Each person sneezed once, when
squirted, and then stood completely
still - like statues.

"Do not be alarmed," Rolzup said. "The
effects are temporary - except you will
not remember seeing the Mother Ship, or
seeing what we are about to do next -
however, you will have happy memories,
which we will share, of all the other parts
of the evening's activities."

We hunkered down in the bushes. That
was why Mavis had told us to hide. The
spacemen never knew we were there.

The Mother Ship projected a green
cone-shaped beam of light down upon
the Flashimoto Tours bus - the bus-
sized one - and we saw it rise up, just
like in a movie. It was tiny, a miniature, next
to the Mother Ship.

Then the spacemen began beaming up.
We saw the first few float up to the

Mother Ship . . . and then we saw Rolzup
bow to Mavis. Mavis bowed to Rolzup. A
green beam of light shone down directly
on her – and we saw our friend float up,
up to the gigantic, hovering spacecraft!

"I must say – I am surprised," Shlermie
said.

XXXIX.

It was the following day. The space-
alien meet had pretty much broken up.
None of the UFO-crazies we talked to had
any memory of seeing the gigantic
spaceship, but they all remembered that
they had a good time and listened to a
great band.

"Come back next month," Rough-Ridin' Rudy
had told them. "We'll have aliens for sure."

We had no idea where Mavis had gone.

XL.

We were sitting in the bunkhouse, not sure what to do. There was clearly no point in reporting Mavis missing and abducted by aliens.

"What do we tell her parents?" I asked.

"Should we wait around for them to bring her back?" Sylvia asked.

"Miss Mavis is a considerate child," Shlermie said. "It would not be like her to leave us without a word."

There was a buzzing noise from Sylvia's backpack. The cell phone!

Sylvia scrambled to dig it out and switch it on. It was Mavis. She sounded scratchy and far away.

"I'll be back before our parents get home," she said. "Meet you in Pokooksie."

"Mavis! Are you okay?" Sylvia shouted.

"I'm having a great time," Mavis said. "I'll tell you all about it when I see you. Meanwhile, remember this: We are not alone! And the others are all fat!"